THE JUNIOR NOVEL

adapted by Tisha West
based on the screenplay by Nick Cannon and Dylan Mulick

Simon Spotlight
New York   London   Toronto   Sydney

This book is a work of fiction. Any references to historical events, real people, or real locales are used fictitiously. Other names, characters, places, and incidents are the product of the writers' imagination, and any resemblance to actual events or locales or persons, living or dead, is entirely coincidental.

SIMON SPOTLIGHT
An imprint of Simon & Schuster Children's Publishing Division
1230 Avenue of the Americas, New York, New York 10020
© 2010 Nick Cannon. All rights reserved.
All rights reserved, including the right of reproduction in whole or in part in any form.
SIMON SPOTLIGHT and colophon are registered trademarks of Simon & Schuster, Inc.
Manufactured in the United States of America 0110 OFF
First Edition
2 4 6 8 10 9 7 5 3 1
ISBN 978-1-4424-0869-2

CHAPTER ONE

Close your eyes and picture the first day of high school. What do you see? Crowds of kids in their newest clothes, trying to impress one another. Boys and girls catching up after the long summer break, talking, texting, making plans. Kids bopping their heads as they listen to their iPods, dancing.

That's what you'd see at most schools. But the Summer Grove Academy for Girls is a whole different scene.

First of all, there are no boys—it's a girls' school, remember? And it's a snooty *private* girls' school, which means there's not a lot of talking, or laughing, or individuality. At Summer Grove, each girl wears the same uniform. Take a look around, and you'll see it's hard to tell a lot of the girls apart. They've got the same golden blond hair, the same shiny faces, and the same fake smiles.

But when you take a closer look, not all of the girls from Summer Grove were cut from the same cookie cutter. . . .

Amanda Rain lazily rolled through the school grounds on her skates. A fourteen-year-old freshman, Mandy—as she called herself—had blond hair like a lot of the other girls, but hers was bleached blond, with bright blue tips. She wore the plaid skirt and white blouse of the school uniform, but with a slight variation: Mandy added a green boy's tie, suspenders, and pink fingerless gloves, and a puff of hot pink tulle peeked out from under her skirt! *Très* chic!

She sat down on a bench and took her journal from her backpack. Song lyrics were scrawled all over the journal cover. So far, the journal was Mandy's favorite thing about Summer Grove. The girls were supposed to use the blank pages to "express themselves." Mandy mostly used hers to write song lyrics and sketch pictures.

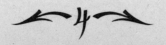

As she opened up her journal, a girl walked past and dropped a flyer on her lap.

> STUNT PARTY AT TEEN ISLAND,
> FRIDAY NIGHT!
>
> KRISTINIA DEBARGE AND
> JUSTIN BIEBER PERFORMING!

Mandy circled the day and slipped the flyer inside her pages. Then she started to write.

Let me lay out the geography of this fine "Institute."

Summer Grove sits approximately 800 meters from the Loyola All Boys Academy. But communication between the 2 species is frowned upon. So the girls' dorms are literally on the other side of the equator from the boys' dorms. Each is protected by evil hall monitors, fire-breathing dragons, and medieval moats.

One PIP thing is that both schools share a main quad, a library, and a football field. So every now and then the prisoners get to graze the same pastures. But . . . NO touching!

Summer Grove has more rules than San Quentin. It's the funniest fun factory in all the land! That's called **SARCASM!**

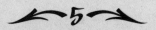

Mandy shut the journal and gazed at the girls walking past her. She was proud of her sense of humor, and she knew some people dug it, and some people, well, didn't.

And she had a strong feeling that the girls at Summer Grove were the kind of girls who just wouldn't get it.

Mandy skated off the bench and kept rolling through the grounds, reading her journal. If she had been paying attention, she would have seen the circle of krump dancers in front of her. But she didn't, so Mandy skated right inside the circle—and smacked into Daisy Johnson.

Daisy was like She-Hulk, an intimidating giant who wore her hair in two puffs on top of her head. She also wore a green sash with the words "Hall Monitor" in white letters emblazoned on it. The sleeves of Daisy's white school shirt were ripped off, revealing her very toned upper-arm muscles.

Scowling at Mandy, Daisy looked down at her combat boots. Mandy's skates had scuffed them.

Everyone felt Daisy getting angry, because when she did, anger seemed to seep out of every pore on her body. And her eyes blazed. Mandy gave her a sheepish smile.

"Nice shoes," she bravely said, before quickly skating away.

Mandy was a newcomer to Summer Grove, but she already knew that it was very dangerous to get on Daisy's bad side. Mandy had actually seen the fierce hall monitor stuff a girl into a locker, blow her ear-piercing whistle right into someone's ear, and hurl a walkie-talkie at a cheerleader's head, taking her down before she could say "Rah!"

Mandy sat down at a nearby bench and continued to write in her journal.

Daisy Johnson is the toughest, hardest hall monitor in the game. Wanted for acts against cuteness both large and small.

She's like the senior gatekeeper, but I think she abuses her power just a tad. And her most gruesome weapon isn't her walkie-talkie, her whistle, or her muscles. Nope. It's her breath! It smells like **HOT GARBAGE**!

Mandy looked up from her journal to see Daisy's face staring right into her own.

"What?" Daisy barked, before Mandy had a chance to turn her head. Mandy nearly passed out from the smell!

In a nearby building, another freshman was doing her own thing. Monica Marriot—known to her friends as Mo Money—sat in front of a vanity mirror. Mo wore the uniform like she was a model on the runway, accenting it with a navy blue vest. As an expensive-looking watch glittered on her wrist, she swiped on some pale gold eye shadow and chatted on her cell phone.

"They don't call me Mo Money for nothing, Paris!" she proclaimed loudly. "Okay, see you next Fashion Week! Kisses to Dolce and Gabbana and Roberto! *Ciao!*"

Tubes and jars of makeup littered the surface of Mo's vanity. The whole setup looked like something from a diva's dressing room, except for one thing: Mo had set herself up in the girls' bathroom.

Outside, a group of angry girls pounded on the door, demanding to get in. But Mo ignored them and brushed her long, wavy black hair. Then she began to write in her journal with a pink pen.

I'm a spender, here, there, everywhere. They say money doesn't grow on trees, yet I beg to differ. You see, money is dollars, and dollars are paper, and paper grows on papyrus trees, of which I have several in my backyard. So as you can see, my logic for excessive spending is supported by scientific fact. Eco-friendly, even!

Some girls are intimidated by the first days of school, but not me. I've a certain "side wah fair" or "genie say quaw," as the French say, which means well traveled and HOT!

People try to "fit in." But not me! Standing out's my MO. I follow the philosophy, "It's not who you know, but who knows you." Therefore, it's my duty for all the PIP girls to know and love me!

The banging on the bathroom door was even louder now, but to Mo it sounded like the paparazzi were trying to invade her space. She smiled at her reflection in the mirror and applied lip gloss to her lips. Then she stood up and started to dance—and why not? She looked too good to sit still!

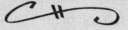

If Mo Money was obsessed with status, she was going to the right school. On the outside, the whole place looked like a fancy country club. There wasn't a single dried-up spot or weed growing on the lush, perfectly cut green lawns. There wasn't a crack in any of the clean white sidewalks that wound between the buildings. Each building was constructed with spotless red bricks.

Jacque Nimble was doing her best to change that. The freshman gave a quick look over her shoulder to make sure she wasn't spotted. Then she started tagging song lyrics on the back wall of the Lockwood Memorial Building with a thick black marker.

Like Mandy and Mo, Jacque had given her uniform a makeover. Her navy blue tie was painted with graffiti. She wore white running sneakers instead of shiny black dress shoes. Her dark brown hair was braided into one long braid that dangled from the left side of her head. Big gold hoop earrings swung from her ears.

Jacque's journal lay on the grass at her feet. The cover was decorated with graffiti designs and cut-out pictures of her favorite rapper, Soulja Boy. A breeze blew open the journal to a page Jacque had been writing in earlier that day.

JACQUE NIMBLE. That's my government. Breaking, freestyling is my politic. Anything hip-hop, then I'm that. Child of the form, student of the game. Got plucked from the hood and shipped here by the man. Ya dig?

Here's the one-two on this place. The organization of the student body at Summer Grove Academy is simple. It's not about what type of person you are, but what type of "girl" you are. Dig? Let me keep it *KRISPY* for you. (And if you're reading this and you don't know what "krispy" is, that means keeping it real, all right?)

You got your jock girls. Your posh girls. Your geek girls. Your tweak girls. You got your ruff girls. Your tuff girls. Your fear girls and your cheer girls. You got your tame girls, game girls, lame girls, and the same girls. The fool girls, cool girls, and the rest are just school girls. All in a constant competition to be recognized. But that's not my style. Yeah, I got skills. But I'm just here to do my time.

Jacque was still tagging the building when one of those girls—maybe *the* girl—stepped up behind her. Bambi Lockwood was the head cheer girl, with long, golden blond hair and a green-and-white cheerleading uniform that fit her body perfectly. It was no coincidence that her last name matched the name on the Lockwood Memorial Building.

Jacque felt the eyes on the back of her neck and turned around. Bambi was not a happy cheerleader.

"You're so gonna love scrubbing that trash off my family's building with your toothbrush, loser," she said condescendingly. "Ugh, the people they let in here these days!"

Bambi blew into the shiny silver whistle that hung from a chain around her neck. Jacque immediately faced the wall, pressing her palms against the brick. She had been through this drill before. . . .

But Jacque wasn't the only girl in trouble. Back in the girls' bathroom, Mo was still dancing in front of the mirror when a loud noise ended her act—a janitor with an ax had busted through the locked bathroom door, followed by a firefighter. Mo flashed them her most dazzling smile, but it was no use.

She was so busted!

Over in another building, Mandy skated into her Home Ec class, hurrying because she was late. Her teacher stood behind a tall cake topped with fluffy whipped cream icing.

Mandy tried to slow down, but she was going way too fast, she couldn't brake in time.

Bam! She crashed right into her teacher, sending the woman facedown into the whipped cream cake. Raising her head, she managed to scowl at Mandy through the sweet goo.

Mandy smiled. "You know what would fix this whole mess?" she asked. "A cherry!"

CHAPTER TWO

At Summer Grove, there was one punishment given to girls who made mistakes like Mandy, Mo, and Jacque: All-Day Detention.

Girls assigned to All-Day Detention, or A.D.D., got stuck sitting in a classroom all day long. There were plenty of rules in A.D.D., and just in case anyone forgot them, there was a big poster on the wall listing all the no's:

> NO TALKING!
> NO WALKING!
> NO WRITING!
> NO MOVING!

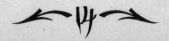

NO EATING!
NO SLEEPING!
NO CRYING!
NO WHINING!
NO SINGING!
NO DANCING!
NO ACTING!
NO SWIMMING!
NO HORSEPLAY!
NO WATER AEROBICS!
NO COOKING!
NO CLEANING!
NO SELF-TANNING!
NO TROUBLEMAKING!
NO **NOTHING!**

Daisy stood outside the door, guarding it to make sure no girl escaped. Inside, Mandy, Mo, and Jacque each sat at a desk, bored out of their minds. The clock on the wall ticked second by second, and it felt like time was moving in slow motion.

Tick . . . tick . . . tick . . . tick . . . tick . . .

Jacque pulled up the hood on her hoodie and put her head down on the desk. Across the aisle, Mo

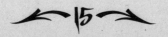

15

aimlessly twirled a strand of black hair around her finger. Mandy sat in front of her, looking from one girl to the next. The boredom was getting to be too much, and she figured the other girls felt the same way. She decided to break the rules—and the silence.

"I got booked on a hit-and-run," Mandy said. "Skated into a cake-clad teacher. It was a sticky-sweet crime scene. You guys?"

Jacque didn't answer, but Mo perked right up. Every diva loves to be interviewed, after all.

"D.W.I.A.! Dancing While Incredibly Adorable!" Mo gushed. "Also known as public displays of awe-someness. Plus tardiness and seizing a school facil-ity without proper permits. Something about a fire hazard."

Mandy was impressed. "Wow, really?"

"Fo sho!" Mo replied proudly. She stood up and nodded to Jacque. "What about you, my hooded friend?"

Once again, Jacque didn't answer.

"Hello? Is anybody home, homey?" Mo asked.

Hearing that, Jacque slowly raised her head and glared at Mo. "I'm here for strangling a nosy posh poser! Cool, *homey*?"

"Uh-oh," Mo said, "Sounds like someone's *mi vida loca*."

Without a word, Jacque jumped out of her seat and lunged at Mo. And she would have gotten to Mo, if Mandy hadn't suddenly gotten between them.

Just then the classroom door swung open. A busty woman in a crisp blue uniform strode in, with two young twin girls. The girls were miniature versions of their mother: same uniform, same perfectly sculpted Afro, and the same tough attitude. Daisy followed behind them.

"What in the name of *Good Morning America* is going on here?" asked Headmaster Jones, putting her hands on her hips.

The twins, Gibby and Gabi, put their hands on their hips too. "Yeah, what in the name of *Good Morning America* is going on here?" they repeated, speaking at exactly the same time.

Mandy turned pale, but Mo wasn't afraid. She stepped forward, smiling.

"Well, Headmaster Jones, we were just . . . dancing! We're working on a new routine, um, for charity," Mo lied. "Baby seal fur coats, I think. Right, ladies?"

Headmaster Jones was skeptical. "Dancing?"

"Dancing?" asked Gibby and Gabi.

The headmaster took a metal ruler out of the leather holster she wore around her waist. She pointed to the sign on the wall.

"Didn't you read the rules?" she demanded.

"Yeah, didn't you?" the twins chimed in.

"Girls, it's okay, cookies, calm yourselves," Headmaster Jones told her daughters in a gentle voice before whirling around to face Mandy, Mo, and Jacque.

"It clearly states dancing is forbidden. This is detention, not *Soul Train*," she scolded.

At that moment a can of spray paint fell from the sleeve of Jacque's hoodie. It clattered to the floor and rolled, stopping at Mandy's feet.

"That's not what I think it is, is it, Jacqueline?" Headmaster Jones fumed. "Tell me it isn't! I said if you were caught with paint, markers, or pencils *not* being used to create a delicate haiku for English comp, I'd send you back to the state facility!"

Jacque looked down at her sneakers. There was an awkward silence in the room—until Mandy piped up.

"Oh, did I just drop my spray can?" Mandy

asked, picking up the can. "How clumsy of me! I, um, we're using that for a science project. Isn't that so?" She glanced at Mo.

"Oh, yes," Mo improvised quickly. "Lava, I believe. Gotta paint that red lava red. Molten red. A beautiful shade! Wouldn't you say, Jacqueline?"

Jacque nodded. "Oh, yeah. Swear to science! Cross my Bunsen burner, hope to transmutate."

Headmaster Jones shook her head. "Y'all must think I just fell off a turnip truck!"

"My goodness, are you okay?" Mo asked, genuinely concerned. "I hate turnips. They're so dangerous!"

Mandy and Jacque giggled quietly. Now the headmaster was clearly confused.

"What? I didn't say—never mind." Then a mischievous gleam shone in her eyes. "Since you ladies are forming such a cute alliance, not only do you have detention together for the rest of the week, but two hours of trash detail every day for a month!" she informed them.

"Wait, trash detail?" Mo asked. "You mean, like detailing my Benz?"

"I don't, Little Miss Fashionista," the headmaster snapped.

A horrified look crossed Mo's face as the truth dawned on her. "You mean trash, like *garbage?* That's disgusting! Can you just expel me, like you were going to do to Jacque? I think that would be easiest on everyone."

Headmaster Jones grinned smugly. She was getting to Mo, and that pleased her.

"Looks like the three musketeers are sticking together," she said. "I'm sure you won't mind sharing our special VIP dorm room then. It's *very* cozy!"

"Yeah. We'll leave the light on for you troublemakers," added Gibby and Gabi.

"So y'all like to start trouble?" the headmaster asked. "Well, my niece Daisy will keep a close eye on you on three. She knows what to do if y'all get out of line."

Daisy was only too eager to carry out her aunt's orders. She cracked her knuckles menacingly. "Yes, Auntie—I mean, Headmaster Jones," she said.

The headmaster made a face. "*What* is that smell?"

Daisy uncomfortably shifted her eyes and smelled her own breath. Headmaster Jones shook her head.

"Daisy, oral hygiene is a friend," she chided.

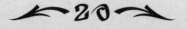

Then with a nod, she ordered everyone, "Outside, now, ladies!"

Headmaster Jones and Daisy marched out the door first, followed by Gibby and Gabi. They smacked Mo on the back of the legs with a ruler as they passed her.

"Troublemaker," the twins called.

"Ouch!" Mo cried. "Please, someone tell me that's illegal."

Jacque turned to Mandy. "Yo, I don't know what's up, but that was cool of you."

"No problem," Mandy said, holding out her hand. "Mandy Rain."

Jacque shook it. "Jacque."

Mo folded her arms across her chest, feeling left out. "Hello! I think my lava paint job had a bit to do with it."

"It was cool of you too, Jane Austen. Quick thinking," Jacque said gratefully.

Mo smiled. "Everybody calls me Mo Money."

Jacque rolled her eyes at Mo's way-too-obvious nickname just as the twins poked their heads back into the room.

"Momma said get outside right now!" they commanded shrilly.

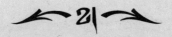

CHAPTER THREE

Headmaster Jones put them on trash duty right away, under the ever-watchful eyes of Daisy, who stood guard on the bleachers. As far as punishments went, this one was pretty bad. Not only did Mandy, Mo, and Jacque have to pick up every candy wrapper, soda can, snot-covered tissue, and bit of discarded food and junk they found, but they had to do it in front of *everyone* at the school field.

Today the bleachers were filled with kids watching the Loyola football players and the Summer Grove cheerleaders practice. Now they had another attraction for their amusement—three freshman girls picking up trash.

Normally, the girls would have been thrilled to be on the field. It was one of the few places on campus where boys and girls were allowed to mingle. But in this situation, having boys around only made them feel much, much worse.

As the girls picked up garbage on the sidelines, they didn't notice one particular boy checking them out.

Justin Lockwood was the brother of head cheerleader Bambi, but the only thing they seemed to share was their family name. He definitely did not share his sister's view of the world, or her sense of entitlement.

Justin skateboarded around the girls a few times, hoping to get their attention. When it was clear that they were too busy picking up trash to see him, he stopped, flipped his skateboard into his hand, and hopped up on the bleachers. He climbed up to where Daisy was sitting.

"What up, D?" he asked cheerfully.

Daisy didn't answer him. Most girls thought Justin was cute, with his tousled brown hair and killer smile, but the tough hall monitor thought he was simply annoying.

Justin ignored Daisy's silent treatment. "Really? That's good to hear," he said, pretending she had answered him. "Got you out here on freshman watch, huh?"

Like the pro hall monitor she was, Daisy kept her focus on the girls. It was as if Justin wasn't sitting right next to her!

"Man, looks like you been in the gym this summer. How much you benching now?" Justin went on.

No reply from Daisy.

"Well, it's always a pleasure talking to you, Daisy. Peace easy!" Justin finished with a grin.

He jumped off the bleachers and skated past the girls once more, and again they didn't notice him.

"I mean, this is kinda awful," Mandy was saying to Mo.

"Kinda?" Mo asked.

"It could be worse," Mandy replied.

Mo held up a disgusting decomposing banana peel. "Really? How?"

Mandy nodded toward the field. "*He* could be out of eyesight."

She pointed to the quarterback of the football team. He looked buff and fit in his green-and-white

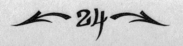

football uniform. A lock of blond hair peeked out from under his helmet, and the blue of his eyes was so dazzling you could see them clear across the field.

"Who's Mr. Hot Stuff?" Jacque asked.

"Colin Andrews," Mo answered.

"Captain of the football team," Mandy added with a sigh.

"And guest star in the hearts of all Summer Grove girls. Mine included," Mo said.

Jacque laughed.

"Uh, I kinda already know him," Mandy said with a coy smile.

Mo scowled. "Yeah, right!"

Mandy got a dreamy look on her face, as she started to tell her story. "It was orientation, a hot, sultry summer afternoon not but a week ago. I was alone, enjoying the light breeze and tender scent of eucalyptus. I wandered the quad near the boys' school. That's where we met."

"You *met* him?" Mo asked jealously.

Jacque was curious. "Yeah, what happened?"

"I'm getting there," Mandy snapped. Then that dreamy look returned. "So, as I was saying. The sun, the breeze . . ."

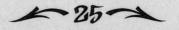

"Yeah, yeah, come on!" Mo said impatiently.

Mandy sighed. "Okay, fine! I was walking along when I happened upon Colin. He was wearing a button-down shirt, top two undone. Anyway, I did something I've never done before. I walked straight up to him! And it all happened so fast."

"What happened?" Mo pressed her.

"I was two steps behind him. He must have heard me because he turned around. And then . . ." Mandy paused.

"And then *what*?" Mo cried.

"And then . . . he sneezed on me!" Mandy added. "It was amazing! His sneeze actually landed on my cheek." Mandy still had that faraway look in her eyes.

Mandy started to make up a song about how Colin sneezed on her. She danced around, pretending her trash bag was Colin. Mo and Jacque playfully joined in. Surprisingly, the girls sounded good together, like they'd been singing together all their lives.

"It was love at first snot!" Mandy said when they finished singing.

Mo giggled. Jacque made a face. "That's the most disgusting thing I've ever heard."

"I find it romantic," Mandy said as Jacque shook her head.

Mo was amused, but not impressed. "Well, Mandy, there's a little competition for those germs," she said, pointing to the cheerleading squad. "Bambi, the pippest girl in a three-hundred-mile radius, head cheer girl, reigning three-time dance team champ. The pip girl that every pip girl wants to be, with the natural ability to crush anyone at will."

The cheerleaders were in a triangle formation, practicing their moves to a new cheer. Everyone looked perfect—perfect long hair, perfect white teeth, perfect fake smile. And there was no doubt that Bambi, who stood in front of the group, leading them, believed herself to be the most perfect of them all.

Jacque recognized her. "Yo, that's the girl who busted me for tagging the Lockwood building. She's the reason I'm on my last strike!"

"Yes, that's Bambi Lockwood, of the Arizona Lockwoods," Mo explained. "They own half the county. Restaurants, malls—she even has her own record label. Her family built this fine academy with money so old it has wrinkles!"

Mandy frowned. "And she dates Colin?"

"She doesn't just date Colin," Mo replied. "She runs his life! Wow, is she my role model. Rumor has it, her old BFF offered Colin a napkin after he spilled some soda on himself one Halloween. One week later, the girl's expelled. Then the next week, she's on a train to some second-rate boarding school when she gets struck by lightning. Her left eyebrow never grew back!"

The football coach blew his whistle, and Bambi blew hers. The football players and cheerleaders headed off the field, grabbing bottles of water and sports drinks on the sidelines. After a while, they all noticed Mandy, Mo, and Jacque. And the girls felt everyone's eyes on them.

"I *can't* be seen like this!" Mo wailed. Without thinking, she tossed her garbage bag over her shoulder. The contents scattered across the field.

Daisy stood up and angrily blew her whistle, pointing at Mo, who cringed with embarrassment. Mandy and Jacque flashed her a sympathetic look.

There was no getting out of it. Mo started to quickly pick up the trash. She reached down to grab a soda can, when another hand touched hers. Surprised, Mo looked up—right into the blue eyes of Colin Andrews.

"Um, wow, thanks," Mo said, blushing.

"No prob," Colin said with a smile. He tossed the can into the bag.

Mo smiled back. "I'm Mo—"

Suddenly a voice shrieked, "Colin! What are you doing?"

Bambi Lockwood stormed up to them, clutching a sports drink in her hand. She was furious. Her best friend, Clair, followed two steps behind her, as she always did.

"I'm just helping this freshman," Colin replied.

"I can see that," Bambi shot back. She snapped her fingers and pointed to the ground next to her. He gave Mo a sheepish smile and walked over to Bambi's side.

Justin, who had been hanging around the field, hoping to talk to Mandy, Mo, and Jacque, finally saw a way to get to know the girls. He went over to Mandy and started picking up trash with her. Bambi frowned at her brother.

"Justin, how can we come from the same

bloodline?" Bambi yelled. "What would Mother say if she saw you here picking up trash with some loser freshmen with major 'wanna-be' complexes?"

"Huh?" Mo asked. Bambi Lockwood was her idol! How could she be so mean?

"Did I stutter, frump-muppet?" Bambi asked.

Mo gasped. Did Bambi just call her a frump-muppet?

Justin saw Mo's expression crumple and jumped in to her rescue. "Be quiet, Bambi, before I tell everyone about that growth you had removed from your neck this summer," he threatened. "That thing had its own facial expressions!"

Everyone giggled—everyone except Bambi.

"Superlie!" she shouted. "You're the one who slept with your Tickle-Me-Elroy toy until you were eleven. Documented fact!"

Now it was Justin's turn to be embarrassed. He turned to Mandy. "That's not necessarily completely true, depending on who and when you ask."

Bambi laughed. When she noticed that Clair wasn't laughing, she nudged her friend, who immediately burst into giggles. Clair did whatever Bambi

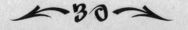

wanted, no questions asked, because as far as Clair was concerned, Bambi was her key to popularity.

"He still plays with toys. But I digress," Bambi said. "I've wasted too many seconds from my ever-eventful life on these bleakburgers. Scenery change!"

With a flick of her wrist, she tossed the red sports drink all over Mandy, Mo, and Jacque. The girls screamed in shock as the sticky, sweet drink doused them.

"Oops! I was aiming for the trash," Bambi said, faking innocence. Then she grinned slyly. "Wait, I think I still got it," she added. "Ha!"

Jacque lunged forward, fists clenched. Mandy and Mo grabbed her arms and held her back. Daisy stood up and blew her whistle, shaking her head.

Jacque gritted her teeth, but she held back. As bad as it was, for some reason, she had changed her mind. She didn't want to have to leave Summer Grove just yet.

Bambi flashed a triumphant smile, turned on her heel, and walked away, with Colin and Clair trailing after her like well-trained puppy dogs.

Mandy turned to Justin and asked accusingly,

"That demon is your sister?"

"Only biologically," Justin replied with a shrug. He was used to his sister's antics, and was resigned to the fact that she was never going to change.

"No offense, but she was half a second away from catching the fist flu," Jacque said.

Justin was hardly offended by Jacque's remark. "Wow, you are a thug for real, huh?" he said, impressed.

Mo Money

Mandy Rain

JACQUE NIMBLE

SUMMER GROVE
ACADEMY

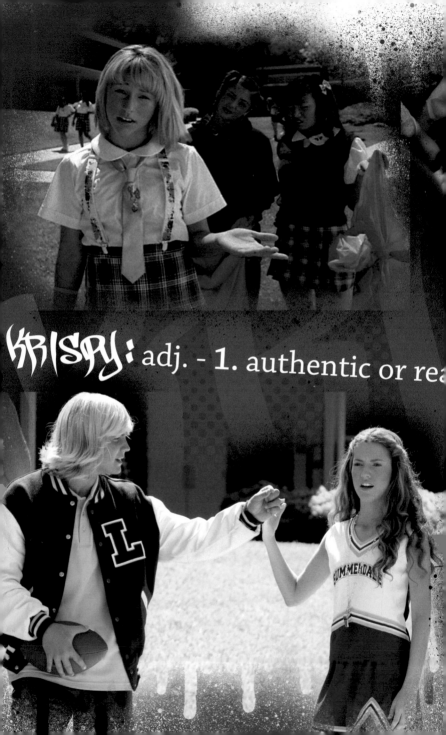

KRISPY: adj. - 1. authentic or rea

2. blunt or straight to my point.

CHAPTER FOUR

Daisy enjoyed her reputation as a tough hall monitor and kept the girls on trash duty for the rest of the day. By the time the sun set, they were tired, dirty, and covered in sports drink stains. Unfortunately for them, the worst part of Mandy, Mo, and Jacque's day was yet to come.

Headmaster Jones had decided the girls should share a room, and Daisy led them to it. They followed her down a dark, deserted hallway to a dented metal door. All of their luggage was piled outside.

The girls looked at one another nervously, each hoping that there had been a mistake in their accommodations. Daisy pulled a skeleton key from her pocket.

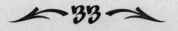

"Welcome to the VIP suite," the monitor announced, as the door creaked open.

Mandy, Mo, and Jacque cautiously walked into the dark room. Somehow Jacque managed to find the chain for the light in the darkness. When she pulled it, a dim light came on, and the girls warily took in their new home.

To call the room seedy would be high praise. It was a dump—only worse. A chalk outline of a squirrel marked the center of the battered wood floor. There was a cot and a set of bunk beds, but the metal bed frames were busted and broken, and springs popped out of thin mattresses. Wind blew in through a broken pane in the only window in the room. Dirt streaked the gray walls, cobwebs hung from the ceiling, and dust bunnies were gathered in every corner.

"This is the headmaster's idea of VIP?" Jacque asked in disbelief.

"Yeah, if by 'VIP' she meant vermin-infested pit," Mandy joked, trying to cheer up the girls.

Mo looked like she was going to faint. "O-M-G! I'm calling my interior designer."

The room was a wreck, but the girls knew there

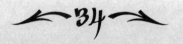

was no way they could convince Headmaster Jones to change her mind. This pit was their home, at least for a while. They dragged their luggage inside and got to work, cleaning the room as best as they could. Mandy scrubbed the chalk off the floor, Mo tacked a sheet over the broken window, and Jacque swept away the cobwebs.

When they were finally done, they showered, unpacked, and put sheets on their broken beds. Then, exhausted, they climbed into their beds and each girl opened her journal.

Jacque nodded to Mandy. "Yo, I think homeboy likes you."

"Colin?" Mandy said hopefully.

"No, Justin," Jacque replied.

Mandy made a face. "Oh, well, um, he's not my type."

"But he's supercute!" Mo cried.

"Have you ever met a guy you *didn't* think was 'supercute'?" Jacque asked mockingly.

"Don't hate just because I'm scoping," Mo shot back.

Jacque shook her head. "Girl, you can't be so thirsty."

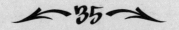

Mandy grinned and looked up from her journal. "What about you, Jacque? Is there anyone you're *scoping*?"

Jacque held out her journal so they could see the cover. "My vision is set high. My dream guy is Soulja Boy!"

"The rapper?" Mo asked.

Jacque nodded. "Yes. Now he's *tamale*!"

Mo started writing in her journal. "*Tamale*. I like that! That's got to go in here. *Tamale*. Of Latino origin, meaning 'hottie.'"

"Hey, I charge extra for jackin' my fresh," Jacque joked.

Mo was impressed. "Another pip phrase. Girl, you are on fire!"

"Yeah, it's like you have your own *slanguage*," Mandy added.

Mo and Jacque looked at Mandy. For a moment, there was an awkward silence. Sometimes Mandy's humor was served with an extra helping of corn.

Then they all burst out laughing.

"Hey, they all can't be winners," Mandy said. "I'm no Bambi Lockwood."

Hearing Bambi's name made Jacque frown.

"Seriously, though, what are we going to do about that Bambi? I can't believe she played us like that. I can't take a whole year of that monster."

"I say we hit her where it hurts," Mandy suggested.

"Now you talkin' my language," Jacque agreed, pounding her fist into her palm.

"I don't mean literally *hitting* her," Mandy said. "I mean taking away what matters to her the most: her popularity. She acts like she runs the school. Let's show her she doesn't!"

Jacque sat up straight. "You mean take her power, and her ego."

"And the whistle," Mandy added. "I hate that sound!"

Mo didn't think taking down Bambi would be so easy. "But she technically does run the school," she pointed out. "Her family's been the financial backers since, like, the Pilgrims and Indians first broke corn husks together. Plus she's head cheerleader, president of every club, and she's won the annual stunt party at Teen Island every year."

"Stunt party?" Jacque asked. "What's that?"

"You know, like Lil' Wayne says, 'Stunting

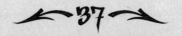

like my daddy!'" Mandy explained.

"A stunt party is like a cool version of a talent show," Mo added. "At the beginning of every year, all the students battle it out at Six Flags on Teen Island night. Dancing, rapping, singing—you can play the ukulele if you want, which I'd advise against. But it's so pip! Thing is, every year Bambi's crowned number-one stunter!"

"Yeah, Teen Island's the who's who spot!" Mandy agreed. "Every celeb, manager, and agent is there on Stunt Night. I even heard Bambi hooked up Kristinia DeBarge to perform this year."

Jacque jumped out of bed. "So that's it! We enter and take her crown."

Mandy and Mo couldn't believe what Jacque was suggesting. The contest was less than a week away. How could they put together an act, let alone beat Bambi?

"Sure," Mandy said sarcastically. "And while you're at it, I'll have a shake with fries and a proposal from Robert Pattinson."

"This is how we teach Bambi what's up," Jacque insisted. "We take what's important to her."

"Um, I have stage fright," Mo confessed.

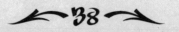

Jacque shook her head. "Don't tell me you guys are scared?"

"No, never!" Mandy cried. "Well . . ."

"It's just . . . ," Mo started to say, but couldn't finish her thought.

Jacque hopped back on her bed. "Good, then we're on. I'm hittin' *Dream* Island. We'll figure out the details in the a.m."

Jacque climbed into her sleeping bag and rolled over, smiling, while Mandy and Mo lay stiff and scared in their beds, their eyes wide open with fear.

What had they gotten themselves into?

CHAPTER FIVE

Another day dawned at Summer Grove, and the campus buzzed with activity as students got ready for their first class.

Mandy left the room first, without skates this time. She wasn't taking any chances.

Jacque walked the halls with her earphones on, scoping out songs the girls could sing at the stunt party.

Mo was the last to leave the room. She had to put her makeup on using the dingy, cracked mirror on the wall, and she kept messing up her mascara.

The hallways were filled with small cliques of girls gathered by the lockers, talking about the latest gossip. Outside, Bambi and the cheer girls watched the other students, whispering and giggling as each one passed by.

Mandy sat on a bench, watching Bambi act like the Queen of Summer Grove. The last thing she wanted to do was get up onstage and sing—but she knew that Jacque was absolutely right. Bambi needed to be taken down, and if somehow, Mandy and her new friends could pull off a miracle, Bambi could lose the stunt party—and a lot of her power.

The first bell of the day rang. Inside her office, Headmaster Jones turned on the microphone on her desk, while Gibby and Gabi stood next to her.

"Good morning, girls!" Headmaster Jones began. Her powerful voice blared from speakers all over campus. "Hope you're having a wonderful first week. For this morning's announcement, I'd like to introduce my spectacular little pumpkin pie orators, Gibby and Gabi! Come on, girls!"

Gibby and Gabi took the mike from their mother. But they didn't *say* the announcements—they *sang* them!

"Good morning, student body, and welcome to the Summer Grove Academy announcements!"

Headmaster Jones quickly took the microphone away from them. "Girls, have you lost your mind?" she snapped. "What are you doing?"

"We're just trying to get an early audition for the stunt party, Momma," the twins said together.

The headmaster angrily shook her head. "Girls, this is a respectable academic academy. This ain't no high school musical. Besides, if you're going to sing the announcements, you sing it like Momma showed you."

She cleared her throat and belted out the lines like a diva onstage.

"Sign-ups for all school cluuuuubs will be in the cafeteria todaaaaaay at La La Lunch! All faculty and student body-ody-ody, please enjoooooy your daaaaaaaaaay!"

Headmaster Jones ended on a high note and turned off the mike. When she faced her daughters, Gibby and Gabi had their hands on their hips.

"Momma, why you always got to stunt?" they asked.

At lunchtime, Mandy, Mo, and Jacque nervously made their way through the lunchroom. There were sign-up tables for student clubs all over the room. Two nerdy-looking girls were playing speed chess at the Chess Club table. A girl wearing goggles and holding a stuffed duck manned the Skeet Shooting Club table. Another girl held out a tray of cupcakes at the Baking Club table. Not a single student was lined up at any of those clubs.

The most popular club was the Dance Club, led by Bambi Lockwood, of course. Small groups of girls hovered around the table, waiting for their chance to impress Bambi. Clair sat next to her, holding a stack of papers.

The lunch bell rang, and Bambi nodded to the cheer girls behind her. They spread out, walking to each corner of the room to stand guard. Clair began walking around the room, handing out flyers for the stunt party. Then Bambi stood up, and all of a sudden, the room went silent.

"Listen up, y'all," Bambi ordered. "You obviously don't need a reminder, but the annual stunt party is Friday night at Teen Island. Dance Club doesn't officially 'sponsor' this event, which I've won the past three years."

Bambi's cheer girls hooted and hollered.

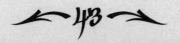

"But if you don't sign up today, you know you ain't stunting on Saturday," Bambi said. "So let's get this going. You have a few more days to hone that talent you've spent all summer crafting, not that it'll help. Anyway, you know the drill. If you think you got skills, sign up here."

Bambi blew her whistle, and the crowds of girls pushed their way to the Dance Club booth. Mandy, Mo, and Jacque got pushed along by the crowd and found themselves facing Bambi.

"Group name and entry fee?" Bambi asked Mandy.

Mandy was too nervous to answer. "I, uh . . . I'm . . ."

"A member of a Dance Team, which is why you're first in line to sign up for the Dance Club. And not some stupid freshman wasting my time, right?" Bambi asked sarcastically.

The pressure was too much, and Mandy and Mo each took a step back. But Jacque wasn't afraid.

"We don't have a name," she said flatly.

Bambi rolled her eyes. "Of course not," she said dismissively. "Well, you can always start with the entry fee. Hundred bucks an act. You can pay for your crew, right, Mo Money?"

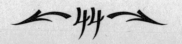

She looked directly at Mo, who shifted uncomfortably. "Um, of course," Mo replied nervously. "I'll just have my . . . accountant wire the funds first thing in the morning. No problem at all, Miss Lockwood."

"So we'll just sign up now, pay later. You got it?" Jacque told Bambi.

"Well, I'm not sure you're on our level of stunting, *Jacko*," Bambi snapped.

"Is that so, *Bimbi*?" Jacque retorted. "We'll show you how we stunt. Get it, girls!"

The challenge was on—right then and there! Mandy and Mo didn't have time to be nervous. Jacque started rapping to a beat she had just come up with.

"What goes around, comes around. . . ."

Mandy and Mo caught each other's eye and began working their best dance moves. Jacque kept rapping, getting right into Bambi's face.

Bambi snapped her fingers, and the cheer girls were instantly by her side. The girls in the lunchroom tapped out a beat on the tables as Bambi and her crew eagerly showed off their moves. There was no doubt the girls were good. Every move was

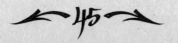

sharp and precise, like a well-rehearsed cheerleading routine.

But Jacque, Mandy, and Mo were no slackers. They countered Bambi's precision team with their own funky moves. They were very good, and Bambi knew it. A dark look crossed her face.

Everyone in the lunchroom sensed the tension. Then suddenly somebody threw a carton of milk in the middle of the dancers, and within seconds, the dance-off turned into a food fight!

Daisy stood against the back wall, calmly watching as apple cores and peanut butter sandwiches sailed across the room. The girls were in deep trouble, but she wasn't about to get her hands dirty.

Until a chocolate pudding cup came sailing toward her.

Splat! It landed on her precious combat boots. Looking down at her soiled shoes, Daisy scowled before stomping over to the beverage table like Godzilla on a rampage. With an angry growl, she flipped over the table.

The girls screamed as a bucket of fruit punch went flying—and landed right on top of Bambi! She

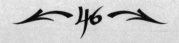

screamed in fury as the sticky punch soaked her.

Mandy, Mo, and Jacque looked at each other and burst out laughing. Everyone in the lunchroom cheered for them, except for Bambi and her cheer girls. Bambi would never admit it, but it was clear to all that she had lost the lunchroom dance battle.

Jacque grabbed a soaked stunt party entry form from Bambi's hands.

"I'll take that!" she said with a victorious smile.

CHAPTER SIX

The girls' lunchroom victory was supersweet, but Mandy, Mo, and Jacque didn't get a chance to celebrate. As soon as the last class bell rang, Daisy herded them straight to detention.

The sound of Summer Grove students talking and laughing in the hallway could be clearly heard in the detention room, and it made the girls' punishment even harder to take. Once again the clock slowly ticked away as they sat there, bored.

With Daisy on guard outside, the girls could at least ignore the "No Writing" rule. Jacque designed new graffiti tags on the pages of her journal. Mandy doodled a cartoon of herself on a romantic walk with someone who looked suspiciously like Justin. Mo, meanwhile, bravely chatted on her cell phone.

"So if you can wire over the funds ASAP, that would be great," Mo said. "And while you're at it, put another thousand extension on my credit card? I saw these new Christian Louboutins online that were to die for. Smooches!"

Mo snapped her phone shut.

"So Mo, we good?" Jacque asked.

"Good and plenty!" Mo replied cheerfully.

"Yahoo!" Mandy cheered.

The door swung open, and Daisy stomped in angrily.

"Did Daisy just hear unauthorized gleefulness up in here?" she asked.

The girls shook their heads.

Not believing them, but having no proof that they broke any rule, Daisy flashed them a warning glare, before turning around and slamming the door behind her.

"How much longer must we endure lockdown?" Mo whispered.

"I wish we could speed up the clock," Jacque whispered back.

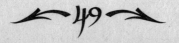

"Speed up the clock." The words sounded to Mandy like words in a song. She wished she could speed up the clock until the next time she saw Justin.

She would never admit it to her friends—and she could barely admit it to herself—but Mandy had been thinking about Justin ever since they'd met. Sure, he wasn't muscular and dashing like Colin, but at least he had the guts to stand up to Bambi. And Mo was right: He was supercute.

Mandy drew another picture in her journal of her and Justin skating through the campus, holding hands. She had to get the cute wave in his hair just right. . . .

"Hello? Did you hear anything we said?"

Jacque's voice interrupted her daydream. Mandy looked up to see Jacque and Mo standing in front of her desk.

"Huh?" Mandy asked.

"We said we should practice our moves low-key for the stunt party to pass time," Jacque said.

"Oh, yeah, I heard you," Mandy lied. "I was just—"

Mo grabbed her journal. "Drawing pictures of Justin. L-O-L!"

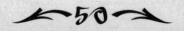

Mandy snatched the journal back. "That is not Justin," she protested. "That's . . . my cousin."

"With hearts and kisses around his head?" Mo asked.

"Uh, close cousins. By marriage," Mandy struggled to cover up, but she knew that the girls wouldn't believe her. So she changed the subject. "Whatever. Let's practice."

Mandy stood up and joined her friends. They quietly pushed some chairs aside and Jacque started to demonstrate some hard-core krumping moves. Mo and Mandy had seen this hip-hop dance style before, but they'd never tried it themselves. In krumping, dancers moved their whole bodies—arms, head, legs, chest, and feet, everything!

Moving to the beat of the music, Jacque started out with some shoulder rolls, rolling her left shoulder forward first, then her right. Mo and Mandy eagerly joined in.

Next Jacque showed them some arm swings, punching the air like a boxer, then crossing her arms in front of each other. Mandy and Mo followed, and the three girls were soon dancing in sync.

Jacque added some foot stomps in time with the

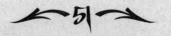

silent beat. The girls got into it, combining all the moves together.

Caught up in the excitement of their dance, they forgot where they were for a moment, and chanted, "Go! Go! Go!"

Oops.

Suddenly Daisy stormed in. "You freshmen just don't listen, do you? I guess Daisy has to teach y'all a lesson!"

The hall monitor put her keys in the lock and locked the door from the inside. The girls were suddenly frightened. What was Daisy going to do to them?

Without saying a word, Daisy cracked her knuckles and backed the three of them into a corner.

"Please don't kill us!" Mandy pleaded. "I never got a chance to experience my first kiss!"

"Shut up and watch this!" Daisy barked.

She swung her arms, but she didn't punch them. Instead, she began a series of truly incredible krump moves. Daisy's moves were fast, exaggerated, and angry. She was a natural. The girls stared openmouthed in awe as Daisy ended her dance with a flourish, stomping her foot right in front of them.

"Now that's dancing!" Daisy proudly declared. "I don't know about that sissy stuff y'all were doing at lunch. But it won't cut it at the stunt party! But you freshmen are probably too scared to really enter anyhow."

"I ain't scared of nothing!" Jacque said, stepping right up to Daisy's face.

"What?" Daisy shouted.

Jacque quickly stepped back, covering her nose. It wasn't that she was afraid of Daisy, it was just that that girl had some bad breath.

"Nothing," Jacque mumbled.

"See, that's y'all's problem," Daisy told them. "Around here, if you start trouble, you've got to finish it."

Daisy stepped toward Jacque menacingly, just as her walkie-talkie beeped. Jacque sighed with relief as Headmaster Jones's voice came over the radio.

"Daisy, I need you in the locker room ASAP," the headmaster said. "The chess team captain got her head stuck in the sink again."

"Roger that," Daisy responded. "I'm on my way, headmaster."

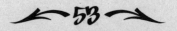

As soon as Daisy left the room and was out of earshot, Mo said, "She needs some serious anger management."

"And a toothpaste smoothie!" Mandy added.

"Can't front, though," Jacque said. "Her skills are dope. And she's right, we can't come soft at the stunt party. We've got some work to do."

Mandy looked toward the door and her face brightened.

"Look, Daisy forgot her keys!" she said. Sure enough, the keys were still dangling from the lock.

"What, you want to escape, McQueen?" Jacque asked.

Mandy's eyes gleamed. "I got a better idea."

CHAPTER SEVEN

Mandy slowly opened the door and looked down the hallway. The coast was clear—no Daisy in sight. She motioned for Mo and Jacque to follow her.

They raced down the hallway, past rows of shiny blue lockers, until Mandy found the room she was looking for: the art room.

Mandy used Daisy's keys to open the door and they stepped inside. The room was a treasure trove of everything they needed to make over their dilapidated dorm room—paint, brushes, buckets, even rolls of colorful fabric. The girls quickly loaded up with supplies and then headed back to their room.

There was a lot of work to do, but the girls were

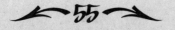

so glad to be free from detention that they were bursting with energy. Mandy started by mopping the grimy floor, sending soap bubbles flying into Mo's and Jacque's hair. When the room was clean, they started to paint everything in sight—the walls, the bed frames, and the rickety wooden desk.

Mandy painted the wall next to her bed bright yellow. As she moved the paint roller up and down the wall, she started to sing.

Mo and Jacque began to dance to the tune, moving to the beat as they painted. When Mandy launched into the chorus, the two girls sang along.

All night, the girls sang and danced as they worked. When they were done, their shabby little room had been transformed into a fly crib.

Mandy had painted a rainbow and clouds on her yellow wall. When the paint was dry, she hung a poster of herself floating in the sky. The wall next to Jacque's bed had a huge Soulja Boy poster surrounded by her own graffiti designs. Mo had painted the wall behind her bottom bunk pink, and added lots of colorful hearts and flowers. The finishing touch was a Mariah Carey poster.

The desk and shelves were painted white and

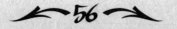

now neatly stacked with their books and school supplies. A rug with a funky circle pattern covered the gray concrete floor.

Finally they were ready to settle in for the night, but they were still too keyed up to sleep. Jacque decided to teach the girls some more dance moves before they went to bed. Mandy got into it, but Mo was distracted. She nervously paced the floor while Mandy and Jacque danced.

"So you saving that first kiss for Justin, huh, Mandy?" Jacque asked.

"Negative," Mandy replied. "How many times do I have to tell you that was—"

"Your cousin," Jacque finished for her. "Why you trying to fake the field goal? You like him."

"If I liked him, I'd tell him," Mandy informed her.

"On that, I have to make a call," Mo said. "Be right back . . ."

After she left, Mandy asked Jacque about Mo, "Have you noticed she's been acting really strange?"

She nodded toward the cell phone that lay on Mo's bed. If Mo was making a call, why didn't she take her phone?

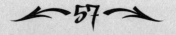

"Don't try to change the subject," Jacque teased. "You like Justin, you like Justin!"

Outside, Mo made her way to the school library. The campus was quiet, and Mo was grateful. She didn't want anyone to see what she was doing.

Mo walked up to the pay phone by the library entrance, inserted some change, and then dialed. "Mommy? Sorry, were you asleep?" Mo said. "Double shifts again. That stinks. . . . Yeah, I kind of need a favor. . . . No, everything is fine. . . . I was just wondering if . . . really, three months late? You had to borrow again?"

Mo sighed and looked down at her feet. "I'm sorry, Mom," she said softly. "I know . . . don't worry about me. You just get some rest. Okay, love you too."

Mo hung up and walked slowly into the library. She didn't think keeping her secret would be so hard. What was the harm in pretending you were something you weren't? Everybody did it one way or another—people colored their hair, or wore clothes to make other people see them a certain way. But it never hurt anybody, right?

Except now, people were going to get hurt. Mo

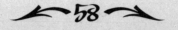

had no idea how to tell her friends the truth. . . .

The sound of an acoustic guitar interrupted her thoughts. She walked to the window and looked out to see where the sound was coming from. To her surprise, she saw Colin playing guitar on a bench outside. He awkwardly strummed a few chords. The song sounded a little mellow and sad—just like the way she was feeling right then.

Mo left the library and slowly approached Colin.

"Hey," she said.

Colin looked up, embarrassed, and quickly put down the guitar.

"Oh, I just found this thing in our dorm," he said.

"I love the guitar," Mo told him.

Colin shrugged. "I'm not really any good."

"What are you playing?" Mo asked.

"Ha! I don't even know," Colin replied. He nodded to some sheets of music on the bench. "I found this music in the library. The cover's gone."

There was an awkward pause for a moment, until Mo broke the silence.

"Thanks for helping with the trash the other day," she said.

"Oh, yeah," Colin replied. "Sorry I couldn't, um, stay."

Because Bambi plays you like a puppet, Mo wanted to say, but she didn't.

"Yeah."

"My girlfriend's kind of . . ." Colin's voice trailed off.

"Whatever," Mo said with a shrug.

"Yeah, whatever," Colin agreed. "I guess. Um, you won't tell her I was here playing the guitar?"

Mo was surprised by the request. "She doesn't know?"

"She knows," Colin said. "She doesn't *approve*."

"What?" Mo couldn't believe it.

"I'm Colin Andrews, the quarterback. Not Colin Andrews, aspiring musician," Colin explained.

Talk about controlling! Mo thought.

"I see," Mo replied. "I won't tell her."

Colin nodded, grateful he could trust her. "Thanks. Mo Money, right?"

"You can call me Monica," Mo said.

Colin smiled. It was a smile so dazzling that Mo actually felt herself blushing.

"I should, um, get going," she said, suddenly

feeling a little shy and nervous. "Kind of a rough night."

"You okay?" Colin asked sincerely. "Wanna talk about it?"

"Not really," Mo replied, although it was nice to be asked. "It's kind of personal, but I'm a big girl. I'll be okay. Take care."

"Okay," Colin said. "Well, good night, Monica."

" 'Night, Colin," Mo replied.

Colin picked up his guitar and walked back to his dorm. Mo stayed on the bench for a while.

She knew she had to tell Jacque and Mandy her secret—or did she? Maybe another lie—a tiny one—could get her out of the stunt party. It was better than everyone knowing the truth, wasn't it?

Then Mo's thoughts strayed to Colin. He was supergorgeous, superpopular, super*everything,* but she felt sorry for him, somehow. Why couldn't he stand up to Bambi? It was sad that he had to play his guitar alone, at night, all by himself.

An idea slowly formed in Mo's mind. Confidence. That's what Colin needed. And if he was confident about his guitar playing, maybe he'd find the guts to tell Bambi to back off. . . .

Mo was so lost in thought that she didn't notice Bambi, hidden in the shadows of the library door. Bambi had witnessed the whole conversation between Mo and Colin, and she wasn't happy.

Mo might have been making plans, but now Bambi had plans of her own. . . .

CHAPTER EIGHT

That night, girls all over Summer Grove Academy fell asleep, dreaming of the stunt party coming up that weekend. But four girls, in particular, were having trouble sleeping.

One of them was Mandy. No matter how much she protested—to her friends and even to herself—Mandy was seriously crushing on Justin. She stared out the window at the stars, and started writing the words to a song about him in her journal.

Then she made up a melody, softly singing the words.

Hearing Mandy's song, Jacque grabbed a paintbrush and, pretending it was a microphone, started to sing along with her friend. But Jacque wasn't thinking about Justin. She was serenading her Soulja Boy poster.

Meanwhile Mo was in the library, walking through the aisles of books, thinking of how she could help Colin, and started to sing her own song about him.

Mo soon found what she was looking for, some books of guitar music. The book Colin was using was worn and ratty. Maybe some of these books would help him be a better player.

The fourth girl who had trouble sleeping was Bambi. She was thinking about Colin too, and about how to keep Mo away from him. She quietly crept up to Headmaster Jones's office and picked the lock with a safety pin. Then she made her way to a row of cabinets and rifled through the files until she found the name she was looking for: Monica Marriott.

Bambi pulled out the file and eagerly flipped through it. A wicked grin lit up her face as she read the contents. She sat at the headmaster's desk and quickly began jotting down notes on a small pad.

Scholarship . . . Parental Work History . . . Past Home Life.

Satisfied, Bambi closed the file and put it back

in the cabinet. Tomorrow, Mo would be sorry she had ever even *looked* at Colin Andrews.

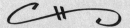

The next morning, Jacque and Mandy waited by Mo's locker, hoping to talk to her about their stunt party routine. Bambi, Clair, and the other cheer girls were hovering nearby. Jacque and Mandy didn't know it, but they were waiting for Mo too.

They didn't have to wait long. Mo strode down the hallway, chatting on her cell phone.

"Beyoncé, I would love to come and sing background for you this weekend. But you know what? Bum city! That means I have to cancel our performance at the stunt party," Mo said, loudly enough so that her friends would hear her. "My girls are going to kill me."

Just then Bambi stepped in front of Mo, blocking her path. Clair stood next to her and started filming Mo with the camera on her phone.

"Can I speak to Beyoncé?" Bambi asked.

"B? Someone wants to speak to you, B," Mo said into the phone. "Beyoncé? Bad signal! The phone on your jet is breaking up. *Hello?*"

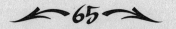

Mo quickly flipped her phone shut. "Dropped call. I hate the phones on the G4s. That's why I prefer to fly G5s personally."

Bambi snatched the phone from Mo's hand.

"Give me back my phone!" Mo yelled, lunging at Bambi. But two cheer girls quickly ran to her side and held her back.

"Clair, are you filming all of this?" Bambi asked.

"Yep. Please believe it," Clair replied.

Bambi tried to dial a number on Mo's cell. Then she grinned and held the phone up to Clair's camera.

"See, just as I thought. Not in service," Bambi said triumphantly. "Her cell phone has never even been turned on. She probably couldn't afford the minutes. So instead she just walks around *fronting*!"

Jacque stepped up to defend her friend. "That's not true, punk!" she told Bambi.

"Oh, yes it is," Bambi coolly replied. "She's been lying to you too, *chica*. She's been lying to everyone! Monica Marriott, from *Rockport*? Not exactly the right side of the tracks, is it?"

Bambi circled Mo like a hawk about to attack a terrified mouse. Mo closed her eyes and wished the floor would swallow her up. Her worst nightmare had come true!

A crowd of girls began to form to watch the scene as Bambi went in for the kill.

"Let's see, your mom is part of the 'club,' that's for sure," Bambi said. "I believe she's taken my diner order a couple of times. Yes, she has. I remember her well, because you both have the same ratty hair and knock-off threads," Bambi said viciously.

Mandy pushed her way through the crowd. She didn't care if Mo had lied. Bambi was going too far.

"And your father?" Bambi went on. "Not exactly a CEO. Not exactly anything, as far as I can tell. I'm assuming he's 'not in the picture.' So sorry for that."

That last remark was so cruel it even made Clair cringe. Mo bravely held back tears, but Bambi wasn't finished yet.

"So what? You do well on a test, get a scholarship, which I'm sure my daddy is paying for, and think you can roll up to a new school *and* a new class?" Bambi asked.

Down the hall, Daisy noticed the commotion and turned on her walkie-talkie to make a report.

Mo slowly backed up as Bambi pressed on her, trapping her against the bathroom door.

"That's not how it works, poor girl," Bambi said.

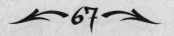

"It's not my fault or responsibility that you've had it rough. The psychologists call it borderline delusional personality disorder. Look, you're *not* like us. And you *never* will be. You are trash. Face it. You don't come to my school and mess with me! You don't front and expect to get away with it!"

Bambi was right in Mo's face now, and this time, Mo couldn't stop the tears from falling down her cheeks.

But Bambi was not done. "And you don't talk to my boyfriend, ever! You smell, your clothes are wack, you're fake, and now everyone will know!" Bambi spat out. "Guess your accountant won't be wiring you the fee for the stunt party after all, huh? You're a sad excuse for a Summer Grove girl. Do yourself a favor and leave . . . like your father did."

Just then Jacque walked up to Bambi and pushed her aside. No one was going to destroy her friend like that! Mo quickly ran away, and Mandy went after her. Bambi glared at Jacque angrily.

"What?" Jacque snapped. "What you gonna do, cheer girl?"

She lunged toward Bambi, but Daisy jumped in to separate the two of them.

"Y'all don't make Daisy get crazy!" she warned.

Bambi glared at Jacque before stalking off. Clair looked embarrassed by the whole thing, but she followed Bambi loyally.

When Headmaster Jones and the twins arrived, the crowd quickly dispersed. Only Jacque remained, still fuming with anger.

"Daisy, I got your call," Headmaster Jones said. "What in the wide world of schools is going on here?"

Gibby and Gabi thought they knew what was going on. "Troublemakers, Momma! Troublemakers!"

"Daisy, tell me what happened," the headmaster said.

Daisy opened her mouth to speak. "Well—"

Headmaster Jones waved her hand in front of her face. "Ooh, never mind. Write it down, child!"

Gibby and Gabi couldn't resist repeating their taunt. They pointed at Jacque. "Troublemaker!"

"Daisy, I want a full report on this incident on my desk tomorrow," Headmaster Jones said, turning to leave.

"Troublemaker," the twins whispered one last time, before disappearing down the hallway with their mother.

Jacque stormed off in the other direction. Somehow or other, Bambi was going to pay for this!

CHAPTER NINE

Mo was too humiliated to go to class. She locked herself in one of the girls' bathrooms. Then she sat on the floor and cried her eyes out.

Jacque sat in computer class, glaring at Bambi and the cheer girls as they uploaded the video of Mo's humiliation onto the Internet. Every cell in Jacque's body longed to stop Bambi, but one more infraction and Jacque would get kicked out of school. Mandy kept an eye on her, making sure she didn't give in.

Bambi's video swept through the school like wildfire. She e-mailed the clip to everyone in her address book. Then those who received it e-mailed it

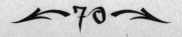

to everyone in *their* address books. By the afternoon, every student at Summer Grove Academy for Girls and the Loyola All Boys Academy had gotten the clip.

Colin first saw it at football practice. A bunch of guys were gathered in a circle, laughing. He leaned in and saw poor Mo's crying face on a cell phone screen. Colin looked across the field and saw Bambi on the sidelines with the cheer girls. She was smirking, obviously pleased with herself.

Justin saw the clip on the laptop in his dorm room, after one of his friends e-mailed it to him. He angrily slammed the lid of the laptop shut before it was finished. He'd seen all he wanted to see, and he was angrier at his sister than he had ever been in his life.

It was night when Mo finally found enough courage to leave the bathroom. But when she got back to the room, she turned on her laptop, only to find that someone had e-mailed the clip to her. She burst into tears once more and then locked the door. She couldn't face anyone—not even her best friends.

Out in the hallway, Mandy and Jacque tried to console her.

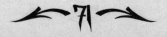

"Come on, let us in!" Mandy said. "No one cares about that stupid stunt party."

"We are your girls!" Jacque reminded her. "You know we got your back."

"Just go away!" Mo shouted.

"Where are we supposed to go?" Mandy yelled back.

"Yeah, this is our room too, you know," Jacque added.

Mo didn't answer, but her friends weren't about to give up.

"Look, we love you regardless of all this drama," Mandy said.

Jacque nodded. "Shoot, we don't care if you're broke. I'm broke too! I like being broke. Ninety percent of the country is broke. It's the hot new thing!"

They heard Mo giggle inside the room, but she didn't budge.

"Well, you're totally the most popular girl on campus," Mandy said, trying to put a positive spin on things.

"And the whole Internet," Jacque added.

Mandy cringed. "You're not helping," she moaned.

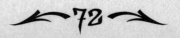

"Shut up, neither are you," Jacque shot back.

Mandy thought for a moment. "I know how to cheer up Miss Thang," she said finally. "Follow me."

Mandy and Jacque snuck down the dark hallways and ducked into the main office. Mandy sat in front of the microphone and turned on the PA system.

"Testing, testing," Mandy said, and her voice boomed over the campus.

Jacque grabbed the mike. "Yo, check this out! This goes out to the freshest, most pip chick in the whole school. My homegirl, Mo!"

Back in the room, Mo couldn't help it, and started to smile. Her girls were the best!

Over in the headmaster's suite, Gibby and Gabi ran to their mother's bed. Headmaster Jones wore a sleeping mask over her eyes and was snoring loudly.

"Momma, wake up!" the twins cried. "Momma, do you hear that? We are being infiltrated! Wake up, woman!"

Back in the office, Jacque yelled, "Hit it, Mandy!"

Mandy started to sing a new song she'd written for the girls. Jacque joined in, and the two girls sang and danced in front of the microphone.

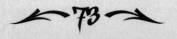

The driving beat and upbeat melody got the sleeping students of Summer Grove out of bed. Girls stumbled out into the hallways in their pajamas for an impromptu dance party.

Mo heard the music and laughter outside the room. Curious, she stepped outside. The dancing girls greeted her with smiles. Mo walked through the hallways in disbelief as the girls cheered her on. No one was calling her a liar or avoiding her!

Back in the headmaster's suite, Gibby and Gabi were about to dump a bucket of water on their mother when she woke up. Ripping off her sleeping mask, she jumped out of bed and heard all the commotion for the first time. Mandy and Jacque's song was blaring through every intercom in the school.

Headmaster Jones was furious! Just what was going on? She hurried to the office to find out.

But as she was on her way, Mandy and Jacque had already finished their song and were heading back to their room. The pajama party was still in full swing. A group of girls crowded around Mo, telling her how sorry they were for what Bambi had done. Bambi had wanted Mo to look like a loser, but Mo was clearly coming out on top.

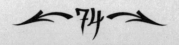

Headmaster Jones and the twins burst into the office, hoping to still catch the singers. But the room was dark and quiet.

They rampaged through the quad, going from dorm to dorm with a flashlight. By the time they reached Mandy, Mo, and Jacque's dorm, all the girls were back in their rooms, and in their beds.

"Something ain't right up in here," Headmaster Jones said suspiciously.

"Troublemakers," the twins mumbled.

Headmaster Jones looked down at her girls and shook her head. "Can't believe you woke me up and we found nothing, girls. I was dreaming about Denzel and George Clooney teaching me how to swim!"

CHAPTER TEN

Mandy, Mo, and Jacque lay in their beds, quietly giggling. Mo was almost feeling like herself again. What had started out as one of the worst days of her life had ended a lot better than she'd ever thought it could.

"Y'all sure know how to cheer a person up," Mo told her friends. "I really love you guys."

"We love you too," Mandy said, looking down from her perch on the top bunk.

"Now shut up and go to sleep!" Jacque said. "Dang, we haven't even known one another a week yet."

Mandy grinned. "That's Jacque's way of saying she loves us too."

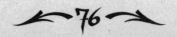

"I know!" Mo said.

They all laughed. Then they heard the sound of pebbles hitting their window. Curious, Mandy climbed down from her bunk and looked outside. A huge smile crossed her face.

"It's Justin," she told Mo and Jacque.

"Great," Mo moaned. "What does he want? An autograph?"

Mandy opened the window.

"Hey," Justin said casually, as if it wasn't the middle of the night and he hadn't just thrown rocks at the window.

"Hey," Mandy replied, trying to sound just as casual, although her heart was thumping a mile a minute.

"Can I, you know, come up?" Justin asked shyly.

Mandy looked at her friends. Mo nodded.

"How are you going to get up here?" Mandy asked Justin. But before he could answer, she had already figured it out.

A few minutes later, Justin was climbing up the side of the building on a rope ladder made of the girls' clothes tied together—jeans, T-shirts, even pajamas. His skateboard was attached to

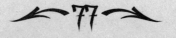

the backpack strapped to his back.

When he reached the window, Mandy grabbed his arms and helped him in.

"Thanks," Justin said. He looked at Mo. "Dude, what my sister did was horrendous, monstrous, completely awful, and wrecked."

Mo smiled weakly. The shock still hadn't worn off.

But Justin grinned and said, "I know just how to get her back!"

The girls perked up. Justin took his backpack over to Jacque's bed and opened it up. He started spreading out a bunch of photos.

"Here's every embarrassing photo ever taken of my sister, Bambi," Justin said proudly.

The girls stared openmouthed at all the photos in front of them. They were truly awful! There was one with Bambi after a spray tan gone wild. Her skin was the color of orange soda! Another picture showed a young Bambi in braces with headgear strapped around her jaw. And then there was the one of Bambi in a hospital gown with a gross-looking boil on the side of her neck.

"O-M-G!" Mandy cried in shock.

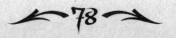

But Jacque was thrilled. "This is *totally* what we need. Look at all this!"

"But what do we do with them?" Mo asked.

Justin clearly had come prepared. "Ladies, mark your calendars and start your engines! We're gonna make some money, more than enough for any stunt party entry fee."

The girls listened as Justin laid out his plan: He would scan the photos into his laptop and use a program to turn them into calendar pages. Justin was sure that every student in both academies would want to have one. So all he and the girls had to do was print out and put together enough calendars to make enough money for the entry fee.

The girls agreed it was a great idea, and they got to work right away. Justin and Mandy designed the calendar pages. Mo handled the printer, and put the pages together. Jacque went out in search of paper for their project. She came back after a short time lugging a huge cardboard box.

"All the paper we would ever need!" she said proudly.

The project took all night. They put together stacks and stacks of the Bambi calendars. At some

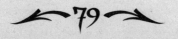

point in the early morning, they passed out on the floor.

Just around sunrise, one of the towering stacks slid into Justin and woke him up.

"Oh man, it's morning," he said, stretching. "I gotta go."

He grabbed a box of calendars and headed to the window. Mandy sleepily raised her head and smiled at him before settling back down to sleep.

"Nighty night," she muttered.

Justin looked back at her and smiled, then hauled himself out the window.

A few hours later, the calendar business was up and running. Mo set up a table right in the middle of the quad and stacked it with calendars.

"Extra, extra, read all about it!" Mo yelled. "Dollar apiece! Sellin' like hotcakes! Get 'em while they last!"

Everyone quickly gathered around to see what all the fuss was about. When they saw the calendars, they squealed with excitement.

Over at the boys' school, Justin skateboarded down the hallways, tossing calendars into dorm rooms as he passed, like a paperboy delivering newspapers. Colin discovered a copy of the calendar in his guitar case, along with the music books Mo had found in the library.

At lunchtime, Mandy went from table to table, making sales.

Jacque roamed around the grounds, approaching any group of girls she saw. She even walked up to the clique of krump dancers and handed one to Daisy. Daisy flipped through the pages and chuckled, then quickly checked to make sure no one saw her laughing.

After school, the girls were back on trash detail. But for once, they didn't mind. Everything was going their way. Not only did they have enough money for the stunt party entry fee, but they'd paid Bambi back big-time for humiliating Mo. They danced as they picked up garbage on the side of the football field.

Across the field, Bambi was holding a copy of the calendar and screaming at the cheer girls. Colin walked over to calm her down, but she screamed even louder. When Justin whizzed by on his skateboard, Bambi's face turned purple at the sight of him. She knew he had everything to do with this!

She threw the calendar at him, then ran after him. Justin easily dodged her and escaped behind the bleachers.

Mandy, Mo, and Jacque watched the chase and high-fived each other. It felt good to be on top for once!

CHAPTER ELEVEN

On Friday morning, Mandy, Mo, and Jacque strode confidently down the hallway to Bambi's locker. Jacque held an envelope that contained one hundred dollars.

Bambi stood by her open locker with a beaten look on her face. Jacque held out the envelope, and Bambi reached out like she was going to take it. Then she stopped. Dropping her hand, she simply smiled at Jacque and shut her locker door.

A man with graying hair and dressed in an expensive suit was standing behind Bambi, having a heated discussion with Headmaster Jones. They were both holding a Bambi calendar. Gibby and

Gabi tugged at their mother's skirt when they saw Mandy, Mo, and Jacque.

The girls froze, terrified. Jacque immediately turned to the lockers and pressed her palms against them.

"Jacqueline, get your butt over here!" Headmaster Jones ordered. "Girls, this is serious, what you did to poor Bambi."

The gray-haired man cleared his throat loudly.

"What you did to the Lockwood family," the headmaster clarified, "is not acceptable. Defamation of character is a serious offense. Not to mention unethical and against the Summer Grove code. I'm putting you three on Superfied Permanent Detention until further notice."

"Oh, Daddy!" Bambi wailed. She ran to the gray-haired man and hugged him. Then she winked at the girls.

Jacque was furious. "What about what Bambi did to Mo? She humiliated her and put a video of it on the Internet."

"I don't know anything about that," Headmaster Jones replied. "But here at Summer Grove two wrongs don't make a right. They make permanent detention."

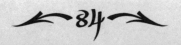

"Headmaster Jones, this isn't fair," Mandy protested.

"Life isn't fair, little one," Mr. Lockwood said cheerfully. "No one defames Clan Lockwood."

Bambi gave her father her best sad-little-girl look. "I am so hurt, daddy. I mean, how am I supposed to bring my A-game to the stunt party tonight?"

Mr. Lockwood ruffled his daughter's blond hair. "Bambilee, you're a Lockwood! A-game is in your blood. And don't you worry, the headmaster will resolve this. I'm sure very quickly too, as the annual fund-raiser is approaching."

He cast a glance at Headmaster Jones, and she knew exactly what it meant. If she didn't come down hard on the girls, Mr. Lockwood's generous donations to the school would dry up.

"Um, yes," she agreed quickly, looking at the girls. "As per Mr. Lockwood's suggestion, the school board and your parents will be notified and brought in for a conference next week. Major consequences, girlies."

Mr. Lockwood beamed at his daughter. "See, who loves daddy's little buttercup? Now you can focus on bringing home the crown yet again, darling."

He and Bambi both raised their right hands, stuck a thumb on one ear, and wiggled their fingers in some kind of goofy family hand signal. But Bambi wasn't finished. She wanted to make absolutely sure that her biggest competition for the stunt party crown wouldn't be there.

"Well, I wouldn't be able to perform if *those three* were there," she said, nodding toward Mandy, Mo, and Jacque.

"They ain't going nowhere, that's for sure," Headmaster Jones said firmly. "These three will be living in detention. And thanks to you, Mr. Lockwood, we have our new super high-tech surveillance system all fired up. Breaking out of detention now will be a mission impossible."

"Well done, Jonesie," Mr. Lockwood said.

The headmaster gave the girls a stern look. "Follow me," she ordered.

Mandy, Mo, and Jacque looked at each other, miserable. But there was nothing they could do.

Headmaster Jones motioned to her twins. "Gibby and Gabi, show Mr. Lockwood to the lobby and his chauffeur."

Gibby and Gabi stepped forward stiffly, like soldiers obeying a command.

"Follow us, sir," they told Mr. Lockwood. Then they cast a warning glance at their mother. "Momma, you be careful with those troublemakers!"

The twins marched down the hallway. As Mr. Lockwood was leaving, Bambi whispered in his ear.

"It was Justin, too, Daddy."

Her father frowned and hustled to catch up to Gibby and Gabi. Bambi flashed a triumphant smile at Mandy, Mo, and Jacque as they glumly followed Headmaster Jones down the hallway.

It *had* felt good to be on top for once—but Bambi had just knocked them right back down, and it hurt. Bad.

CHAPTER TWELVE

The scene at Six Flags that night was off the chain as the Teen Island stunt party geared up. Bright lights flashed on and off, illuminating the stage where the acts would perform. Roadies set up amps, microphones, and drum kits. Above the stage hung a sign with the colorful Teen Island logo, a round robot-looking dude sporting headphones.

Kids swarmed to get the best places by the stage. Others lined up to grab some food at one of the snack bars. Flashbulbs popped as the paparazzi swarmed around the arriving celebrities. A DJ on the side of the stage started spinning records, warming up the growing crowd.

Every teen within a hundred miles was heading for the stunt party—that is, every teen except Mandy, Mo, and Jacque. The girls sat in the detention room, forlornly gazing out the window at the starry night sky.

It had been a long week. They had bravely sung and danced their way through trash duty and detention. They had transformed a dungeonlike dorm room into a cool crib. They had saved Mo from humiliation and given Bambi a taste of her own medicine.

But it had all been for nothing. The girls' spirits were broken.

"Well, we tried," Mandy said with a sigh. "I guess I'd better start scoping out a new school."

"When my guidance officer hears about this, I'm sure it's back to the state facility for me," Jacque said, putting her head on her desk.

"I feel like all of this is my fault," Mo said sincerely. "I'm sorry I got you guys into this mess."

"Girl, it ain't your fault!" Jacque said. "This is all for one and one for all."

"Exactly," Mandy agreed. "I don't know about y'all, but this has been the most exciting first week of school ever."

Jacque sat up straight. Her brown eyes shone with determination. "Well, I say we keep the excitement rolling!" she said. "These four walls can't hold us! We can't take this sitting down. We got a stunt party to win! If we got to go out, we got to go out with a bang."

"Yeah!" Mandy cheered.

Jacque shushed her.

"Sorry, I mean, 'yeah,'" Mandy said in a whisper.

"But the stunt party has already started," Mo pointed out.

"So that means we have no time to lose," Mandy said.

Jacque nodded. "Let's put our heads together and devise a plan."

The girls pushed their desks together and opened their journals.

"All right," Mandy said. "First things first. We're locked in here."

Jacque held up a paper clip. "No problem."

"Check," Mandy said, writing in her journal. "Then there's the new high-tech surveillance system. Video cameras in the hallway, laser-activated alarm system."

"And don't forget Daisy by the front door of the building," Mo reminded them.

"And once we're out, we'll need a way to get to the stunt party," Jacque added.

"No problem," Mandy said confidently. She already had an idea. "We can handle this."

They talked excitedly for a few minutes, figuring out their plan. Soon they were ready to take action.

"Let's do this," Mandy said, standing up.

First, Jacque picked the lock to the door using the paper clip. The door swung open, and the girls cautiously walked out, peeking down the hallway to make sure no one was around.

Spotting the surveillance cameras, Jacque took a can of spray paint from the pocket of her hoodie. She reached up and quickly shot paint into the lens of one of the cameras.

"Next phase," Jacque said casually. So far so good!

They tiptoed down the hallway where, close to the front entrance, there was a pattern of green laser beams crisscrossing the hall and blocking their way out. If one of the beams was touched, an alarm would sound. And they'd be in even worse trouble!

"Me first," Mo bravely volunteered.

Mo cartwheeled over the first beam, then flipped over the next, then somersaulted and slid under the last beam to safety. Mandy and Jacque followed. The girls didn't hit a single beam!

Jacque hit the next video camera with a shot of spray paint. The girls nodded to one another.

"Next up, Operation Daisy," Mandy said.

Daisy stood guard just outside the front door. She wasn't thrilled about missing the stunt party, but she was a hall monitor, and she had to do her duty, no matter what.

Suddenly Daisy heard a creak behind her and turned around. She pointed her flashlight toward the noise, but saw nothing. Then she heard another noise, and flashed a beam of light in that direction. Still nothing. Daisy was getting annoyed.

Then she spotted something on the floor next to her foot—a giant pack of gum! Where did that come from? She bent down to pick it up . . . and it moved! Now these weird goings-on were going a bit too far.

She reached for the gum again, and it still slid away from her. Angry, Daisy chased after the gum.

Little did Daisy know that down the hallway, Mandy, Mo, and Jacque were using an invisible fishing line to pull the gum away from Daisy. The girls stifled their giggles as the hall monitor followed the gum right into a storage closet, just as they had planned.

Once Daisy was in the closet, the girls quickly got to work tying her to a chair. Their determination to get to the stunt party made them forget how afraid they had been of the hall monitor. And Daisy herself was so shocked by the girls' actions that she forgot to fight back.

When the girls were sure that Daisy was securely tied up, Jacque took a bunch of gum and stuffed it into Daisy's mouth, before taping her mouth shut.

On to the next phase! The girls quickly raced through the front door, and into the parking lot. They had made it! They ducked down and made their way from car to car like ninjas on the move.

Suddenly, bright lights shone at them, and the girls froze. Then a friendly, familiar voice rang out.

"Hey, it's me," Justin called.

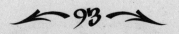

The girls ran up—and found Justin driving a golf cart. They eyed it suspiciously, but got in anyway. Mandy climbed in next to Justin, and Mo and Jacque sat in the small backseat. The golf cart began to putter out of the parking lot.

"Thanks for coming," Mandy said.

"No problem," Justin replied.

Jacque frowned. "I thought you said you had a car."

"Correction, I said I had a fly ride," Justin pointed out. "I don't get my driver's license for another two years, so this is the next best thing."

"I like it!" Mandy said.

"It only goes five miles an hour!" Mo complained.

Jacque shook her head. "I know eighty-year-old ladies who can run faster than this thing."

"We're never gonna get to stunt at this speed!" Mo wailed.

CHAPTER THIRTEEN

Over at Teen Island, the stunt party was in full swing. The MC got onstage to announce the first act.

"Everybody give it up for our first stunner of the night, Baby Dulow!"

The crowd cheered as an eight-year-old boy ran onstage and started to rap. It was a high-energy start to what promised to be a wild night. Baby Dulow was followed by a team of break-dancers, a rock band, and a hip-hop act. Then Headmaster Jones appeared, dressed in a long, colorful '70s-style orange and pink dress with a paisley print. Behind her, Gibby and Gabi were dressed just like her, each holding a bass guitar.

"I know what y'all are asking, what is the head-master doing onstage?" Headmaster Jones boomed into the mike. "But I wasn't gonna miss this for the world. My little girls are stars! Hit it, Gibby and Gabi!"

The twins started to lay down a funky bass beat, joining their mother in singing a soul tune. The crowd cheered them on.

Meanwhile, Mandy, Mo, and Jacque were still miles away. The golf cart slowly cruised along the side of a street.

"Trust me, we'll make it," Justin assured them. "My sister always makes the party run fashionably late."

"So what happened when your dad found out about the calendar?" Mandy asked.

"He threatened me with military school," Justin replied. "But he changed his mind when I mentioned a secret of his, and he even gave me twenty dollars."

Mandy laughed. She was happy to be next to Justin, no matter what happened. In the backseat, Jacque and Mo were getting impatient.

"Are we almost there yet?" Jacque asked.

"Yeah, chill, we're down the street," Justin answered. "Only, like, twenty more miles."

The girls groaned. At this rate, they would never make it!

Back on Teen Island, Bambi stood backstage with her cheer girls. Instead of their usual cheer uniforms, the girls were dressed for the stage in supershort sequined black shorts, sparkly black tank tops, and white collars to give their costumes a tuxedo effect. Knee-high white patent-leather boots finished the look.

Bambi was feeling great. She and her girls looked fabulous. The party was a huge success, as always. And those annoying freshman girls were locked up far, far away.

The crowd cheered again as the MC brought up the next act.

"Ladies and gentlemen, make some noise for the Calvillo Girls!"

The crowd roared as three beautiful, dark-haired sisters stepped onstage. They started singing a bouncy pop song in perfect harmony, and their dance moves were hot. Bambi frowned and turned to her crew. She decided they needed a pep talk.

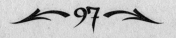

"Okay, ladies, this is our major competition," she said sternly. "They are good, so we have to step it up. This is *my* stunt party and there is *no way* I'm going to let someone outstunt *me!*" Then, catching a few raised eyebrows from her cheer girls, she quickly added, "I mean, *us.*"

The cheer girls shrugged. It was *always* all about Bambi, wasn't it? But they knew that already, and each had her own reasons for sticking with her.

While Bambi eyed the Calvillo sisters, the girls and Justin were slowly getting closer. They'd been in the golf cart for hours! In the backseat, Mo and Jacque leaned on each other for support.

"I'm cold," Mo complained.

"And I'm sleepy," Mandy said with a yawn.

"And I'm—" Jacque began.

"Let me guess, Grumpy?" Justin teased. "That makes me Snow White, huh?"

"Well, Snow White, we got an hour before the party ends," Jacque retorted.

Justin pressed harder on the gas pedal, but the golf cart only slowed down in response.

"Why are we slowing down?" Mandy asked, just before the golf cart came to a complete stop.

"Uh, I think we just ran out of gas," Justin replied.

"You didn't fill up before you left?" Jacque asked in disbelief.

"Yeah, but I guess you didn't notice that this is a golf cart," Justin said sarcastically. "This trip is much longer than eighteen holes."

Mo buried her face in her hands. "We are so going to miss the whole party. This is pointless!"

"Everyone just relax," Mandy said calmly. "We'll figure something out. Justin, since you got us this far, any suggestions?"

"Um, girl power?" Justin asked hopefully.

The girls rolled their eyes. Then they climbed out of the golf cart, and did the only thing there was left to do.

They got behind the cart, and started to push. . . .

CHAPTER FOURTEEN

At Teen Island, the MC stepped back onstage. "All right, time for our next stunner," he announced. "Representing for the Loyola Cubs. Y'all make some noise for your quarterback, Colin Andrews!"

Colin walked out onstage with his guitar strapped over his shoulder. The girls in the audience squealed at the sight of him. Colin's shaggy blond hair hung over his eyes, and he looked supercute in a white button-down shirt, skinny black tie, gray vest, and jeans.

But while all the other girls were excited to see Colin, Bambi was fuming. "What in the world is Colin doing onstage?" she yelled. "Who signed him up for this? Because I sure didn't!"

Clair raised her hand, holding in a smile. She knew Bambi wouldn't like it if Colin performed, but Clair had signed him up anyway. She thought he deserved a chance.

"Well, whatever," Bambi pouted. "If he wants to be a loser tonight, he can go right ahead."

Colin gazed out at the audience. "I want to dedicate this song to a special person tonight," he said. "She inspired me to get up here and do this. But I don't see her in the crowd. Anyway, here it goes."

Colin began to strum his guitar. After Mo had passed him those guitar books from the library, he had practiced every chance he could. It showed. He sang a simple but sweet ballad, and everyone loved it. Nobody had any idea he could sing! The applause for him was loud and long, and Colin left the stage beaming.

The MC came back to announce the next act. "All right, now it's time for the stunner queen! Y'all make some noise for Bambi Lockwood!"

Bambi strode out confidently, followed by her crew of cheer girls. The music started, and Bambi began to belt out her song.

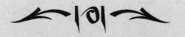

The girl wasn't all talk. She was definitely good. She commanded the stage with the power of a diva. Her voice was strong, and her moves were smooth. When the song finished, the crowd went absolutely crazy.

"Wow! Bambi blazed it!" the MC gushed. "I know I wouldn't want to be one of the judges tonight. But while they deliberate, let's take the party to another level. First, give it up for Island Def Jam's singing sensation Kristinia DeBarge!"

The crowd hollered and clapped as a gorgeous girl with long brown hair took the stage. She entranced the crowd with her own soulful brand of pop music. Everyone in the crowd danced and sang along.

"Amazing!" the MC cried when Kristinia was finished. "And we're not done yet. Give some love to teen singing sensation Justin Bieber!"

The high-pitched shrill of crazed teenage girls filled the air as Justin took to the stage in a black T-shirt and jeans. Two hip-hop dancers backed him up. And when Justin started to sing, the girls screamed even louder.

When Justin's song ended, the MC and Kristinia

came back onstage. The MC was holding a huge gold trophy, and Kristinia held a large bouquet of roses.

Kristinia took the mike first. "And the winner of this year's stunt party is . . ."

"Bambi Lockwood!" the MC cried, and the crowd went wild. "Once again, she is our number-one stunner!"

Bambi walked out onstage, beaming, and took the trophy and the roses.

While Bambi was basking in the glory of victory, the girls were still pushing the golf cart not far from Teen Island.

"Look, I see it!" Justin said, pointing. "Teen Island is just up the hill! Come on, y'all, push faster. We're almost there!"

The girls looked at one another and stopped pushing.

"Let's get it, girls!" Jacque cried.

With a loud whoop, the girls ran toward the amusement park, leaving Justin at the bottom of the hill.

"Hey, what about me?" he yelled. "Y'all just can't leave a playa hanging!"

The girls were out of breath by the time they

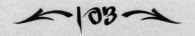

reached the park entrance—and they were too late. The stunt party was over. Crowds of kids were spilling out into the parking lot.

"All this work and we missed it!" Mandy wailed. "This is so lame!"

"Lame is right!" a voice mocked. The girls whirled around and saw Bambi and her crew standing behind them.

"Somebody alert the bounty hunters," Bambi said. "Looks like some fugitives have escaped the loser bin!"

Jacque took a step forward. "I should take that trophy and—"

"Whatever, little gangster girl," Bambi snapped. "I'm tired of your little 'tude. I'm not scared of you or your 'hood.' So you go ahead and try it! You don't want none of Bam-Bam!"

Furious, Jacque took off her earrings and rolled up her sleeves. "It's on!" she yelled.

Mo stepped in front of Jacque. "Fall back, Jacque. I got this," she said.

"Ha, got what?" Bambi asked.

Mo took a deep breath. Jacque was a good friend, but Mo couldn't let Jacque defend her forever. She

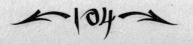

knew she had to stand up to Bambi on her own.

"Look, Bambi, I've learned a lot about life in the past few days," Mo began. "The things I thought mattered really don't. Life isn't about being popular or having money. It's about embracing who you are. Not material things or what people say about you, but who you really are inside. And you know what? I don't think you really know who you are."

Bambi shook her head. "Can you believe this freshman is getting all *Seventh Heaven* on me?" she asked. "Save it. I'm superpip! I'm the best and this trophy only validates that."

"I can't believe I really wanted to be like you," Mo said.

"You couldn't be like me even if you had my money, my looks, my swag, or my boyfriend," Bambi shot back.

A week ago those words would have made Mo cry. Now she just smiled.

"That's fine, because I'm just happy being Monica."

"Tell her, Mo!" Mandy cheered.

"Yeah, and it's too bad you conned us out of competing tonight," Jacque said. "Because you might

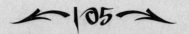

not be walking around with that trophy all prissy if we had."

"Too bad for *you*," Bambi replied. "I would have loved to have humiliated you scrubs tonight."

At that moment Justin showed up. Holding a megaphone, he shouted, "It ain't too late! Let's take it to the concrete!"

CHAPTER FIFTEEN

Word quickly spread through the parking lot that the girls and Bambi were about to face off in a challenge. Cars formed a large circle in the parking lot, then beamed their headlights to form a circular battleground. A huge crowd formed around the circle as everyone waited for the action to start.

Justin stood on top of the golf cart and MC'd through the megaphone.

"It's all about to go down!" he yelled. "Y'all give it up for some real stunners: Mandy, Mo, and Jacque—the School Gyrls!"

Justin had made up the girls' name on the spot, but it fit. The girls still wore their uniforms, not

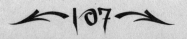

fancy costumes like Bambi and her crew. They jumped into the circle and began to sing.

The crowd applauded loudly as the girls launched into the dance routine they'd been working on in their dorm room. Then Bambi and her crew stepped up. They danced together, and their moves were tight. The dance battle was neck and neck.

Then both crews marched back to the edge of the circle. It was time for each girl to face the others individually. Mandy went first, infusing her moves with her colorful personality. Bambi countered with some perfect steps, but compared to Mandy's, they were tired.

Mo stepped into the circle next, and her moves were sharp and sassy. Bambi tried to outdiva her, but she ended up just looking phony.

Finally it was Jacque's turn. She busted into a hard-core break dancing routine, starting out by top-rocking to the beat with her hands and feet. Then she dropped and planted one hand on the ground, spinning her feet in a circle. She jumped up into a one-armed handstand, then flipped back and landed between Mandy and Mo. The girls stepped back, twirled around, and struck a pose.

Everyone went bananas, clapping and cheering! It was clear who came out on top. The School Gyrls hugged one another and jumped up and down, while Bambi walked back to her crew, defeated. Bambi picked up her trophy and motioned to her cheer girls to follow her. But Colin stepped up and took the trophy out of her hands.

"What are you doing?" Bambi shrieked. She couldn't believe Colin was turning against her!

Colin ignored her. Everyone knew that the School Gyrls had won the battle fair and square. He handed the trophy to Mo.

"You deserve this," he said. "And this."

He kissed Mo on the cheek. Bambi started to stomp toward them, but Justin stepped in her path.

"You don't want to do that," he said. "Trust me. I have plenty more incriminating pictures and lots more paper."

Bambi stormed away, yelling, "Where is the headmaster? I'm telling!"

Mandy walked up to Justin. "I like how you got our backs," she said gratefully.

"Don't I deserve something?" Justin asked, pointing to his cheek.

Mandy blushed. "I guess you do."

She leaned in to kiss him on the cheek, but he turned his head at the last second, and their lips met. Mandy couldn't believe it. Her first kiss!

Jacque watched her friends. She was happy they both got to connect with their crushes, but a little sad that she'd never get to meet her own dream guy. Then she felt a tap on her shoulder. Jacque turned around, and saw Soulja Boy standing there! Beautiful brown eyes, killer smile—and he was *real*, not a poster!

It was too much for Jacque. She fainted, but fortunately Soulja Boy caught her in his arms.

"Uh, are you okay?" he asked. "I just wanted to say I like your dancing. I need to rock some of those moves! Uh, wake up? Hello?"

Mandy and Mo ran up and grabbed Jacque by the arms. Soulja Boy shrugged and walked off as Headmaster Jones appeared on the scene with Gibby and Gabi.

"We have to say, you troublemakers got skills," the twins said.

"Yes, but once again you three have broken major rules," the headmaster said sternly.

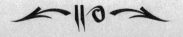

"I'd say 'fractured' more than 'broken,'" Mandy said helpfully.

"So are we kicked out of school?" Jacque asked. "Need I assume the position?"

Headmaster Jones looked thoughtful. "Well, after reviewing Daisy's report I think expulsion is a little harsh. But I definitely think y'all gonna get even better acquainted with that detention room over the next semester."

Bambi ran up to the headmaster, frantic.

"You mean you aren't going to expel them?" she asked in disbelief. "Wait until my father hears this!"

"Wait until your father hears about all the trouble *you've* been causing at the academy," Headmaster Jones warned. "I got you on breaking and entering, theft, threatening students. . . . Shall I continue?"

Gibby and Gabi folded their arms and glared at Bambi. "Yeah. Shall she continue?"

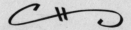

Mandy, Mo, and Jacque sat on a curb and watched as the parking lot emptied out. Mandy held the stunt party trophy.

"I have to say, I think you guys are the first real friends I've ever had," Mo confessed.

"BFFs for real!" Mandy agreed.

"Yeah, yeah, yeah," Jacque said. "That's all peaches and ice cream, but how are we getting back to the academy?"

As soon as the question popped out of her mouth, a black limousine pulled up next to them. The tinted windows rolled down to reveal Justin in the backseat—with Soulja Boy!

"Yo, me and my homey want to know if y'all need a ride," Justin said, grinning from ear to ear.

Once again, Jacque fainted. Mandy and Mo shook their heads and carried her into the limo. Then they loaded up the trophy and headed back to Summer Grove Academy.

The School Gyrls were on top—and heading home in style!

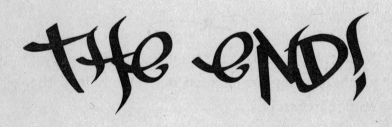

THE END!